This book belongs to
To Kenny

For wonderful Lisa,
an inspiration to us all

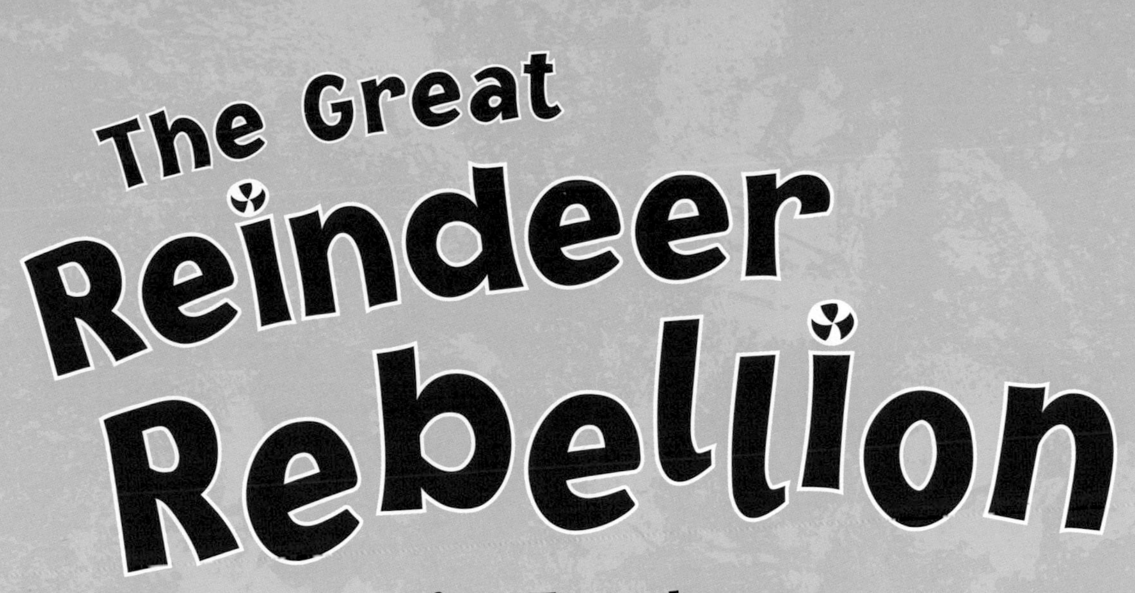

written by Lisa Trumbauer

illustrated by Jannie Ho

STERLING CHILDREN'S BOOKS
New York

'Twas the week before Christmas,
and somewhere up North,
dear Santa was frantic—
he paced back and forth.

He had just heard some news
that he sure didn't like:
It seemed that the reindeer
were going on strike.

Yes, Dasher and Dancer,
and Prancer and Vixen;
even Comet and Cupid,
and Donner and Blitzen!

They said, "We are finished!
We've had quite enough
of pulling your sleigh with
such big, heavy stuff!"

"We're striking, dear Santa,
and until things get better,
no pulling or flying—
we're in this together!"

So Santa decided,
"That's fine! Be that way!
I'm sure I'll find others
who *will* pull my sleigh."

He wrote up a want ad
for lands far and near—
"Please come and help Santa!
Or no Christmas this year!"

Soon creatures came running
and leaping and clomping,
hopping and flying,
and creeping and romping.

"So many to choose from!
Which one should I pick?
I'll show those ol' reindeer
they can't stop Saint Nick!"

"Let's start with the pooches.
Yes! Dogs would be best!"
Then he hooked them all up,
and he gave them a test.

"To the top of my wall!
To the top of my roof!"
And the dogs started scrambling
and barking, "Woof! Woof!"

"They're flying! I knew it!"
Saint Nick began yelling.
But then those eight dogs started
sniffing and smelling.

"There's food!" the dogs whimpered.
"Yes! Food! Come this way!"
And the dogs scampered off,
forgetting the sleigh.

"I won't be discouraged.
Come on, cats! It's showtime!"
The cats trotted over,
and were harnessed in no time.

"Go! Fly!" Santa hollered.
"To the top of that hill!"
So the cats all dashed forward
and they'd be running still . . .

. . . if not for the stray mouse
that ran in their way.
They shook off the harness.
No flying today.

"No pooches, no felines,
what am I to do?
How 'bout some true flyers?"
Called Santa, "Yoo-hoo!"

"Flamingos!" he summoned,
"It's your turn, let's go!
And I must say your pink
looks divine in the snow."

They soared up to the roof,
where they gracefully perched.
"You've got it!" said Santa . . .

. . . but they started to lurch.

On one leg they wobbled,
and hobbled and slipped up.
They soon lost their balance.
Oh! How they tipped up!

Just then came eight hopefuls,
a-hopping along.
"I think we can help, and
we're all very strong!"

"Yes, yes!" welcomed Santa.
"I think you will do!"
Then he harnessed them up,
those eight red kangaroos.

"That's it!" declared Santa.
"You're hired! Let's go!"
But the hoppers soon struggled;
they started to slow.

They stopped, then they stumbled.
They looked quite ashamed,
for their pouches were loaded!
(This weight was to blame.)

"We took all your presents,"
the red 'roos said sadly.
"We're sorry, dear Santa,
for behaving so badly."

And then Santa heard it—
a trumpeting sound,
as eight marching elephants
shook up the cold ground.

"Good fellow, we'll help you.
We're sturdy and steady."
So he harnessed them up and
the great beasts were ready.

They stomped, then took off.
Nick said, "You can do it!"
They sailed to the rooftop . . .

. . . and then fell right through it.

"You're too heavy!" griped Santa,
as he helped them to stand.
"ISN'T ANYONE OUT THERE
WHO CAN GIVE ME A HAND?"

"no sniffers, no chasers,
no animal grouches.
no one-legged birds and
no creatures with pouches!"

Well, who should come over
but the reindeer. How strange!
“We’ll help you, dear Santa,
but a few things must change.”

"A whirlpool and sauna
would make us quite able.
And real beds, not grass, AND
a heater—and cable."
MILK
PRANCER
COCOA

"You will have it, and more!
That's a promise—a fact!"
Then the reindeer and Santa
signed a lifelong contract.
Frosty the Snowman!
LIVE
TV Guide

And that's how it happens
that near Christmas Day,
you'll always see Santa,
and pulling his sleigh
are eight trusty reindeer
who love being in flight.
"Merry Christmas to all!
And to all a good night!"

MILK

To Meredith, for making all the right suggestions. Thanks! —J. T.

To Math Boy Kun, with love. —J. H.

STERLING CHILDREN'S BOOKS
New York

An Imprint of Sterling Publishing
387 Park Avenue South
New York, NY 10016

STERLING CHILDREN'S BOOKS and the distinctive Sterling Children's Books logo
are trademarks of Sterling Publishing Co., Inc.

Paperback edition published in 2014.
Previously published by Sterling Publishing Co., Inc.
in a different format in 2009.

The artwork for this book was created digitally.
Designed by Jannie Ho

Library of Congress Cataloging-in-Publication Data

Trumbauer, Lisa, 1963-
The great reindeer rebellion / by Lisa Trumbauer ; illustrated by Jannie Ho.
p. cm.
Summary: In verse reminiscent of "'Twas the Night Before Christmas," tells of the year
the reindeer went on strike, forcing Santa to audition a series of other animals to take over
their job.
ISBN 978-1-4027-4462-4
[1. Stories in rhyme. 2. Christmas--Fiction. 3. Santa Claus--Fiction. 4. Reindeer--Fiction. 5.
Animals--Fiction. 6. Humorous stories.] I. Ho, Jannie, ill. II. Title.
PZ8.3.T753Gr 2009
[E]--dc22

2008047458

Distributed in Canada by Sterling Publishing
c/o Canadian Manda Group, 165 Dufferin Street Toronto, Ontario, Canada M6K 3H6
Distributed in the United Kingdom by GMC Distribution Services Castle Place, 166 High Street,
Lewes, East Sussex, England BN7 1XU
Distributed in Australia by Capricorn Link (Australia) Pty. Ltd.
P.O. Box 704, Windsor, NSW 2756, Australia

ISBN 978-1-4549-1356-6

For information about custom editions, special sales,
premium and corporate purchases, please contact
Sterling Special Sales Department
at 800-805-5489 or
specialsales@sterlingpublishing.com.

Printed in China

Lot #
2 4 6 8 10 9 7 5 3 1
05/14

www.sterlingpublishing.com/kids